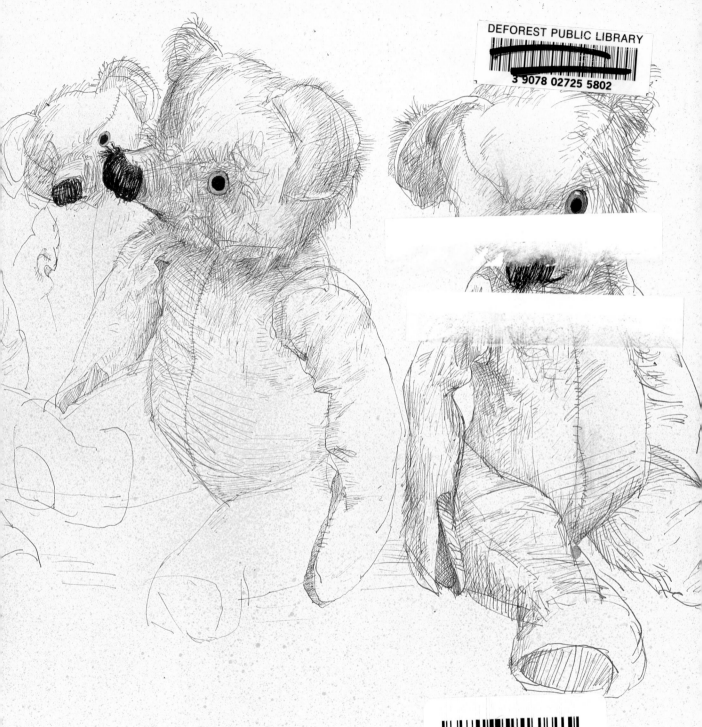

FOR GRACE VICTORIA
and
REBECCA SCARLETT

WHOOPEE!!

TeDDY! WHERE ARE YOU?

Ralph STEADman

Andersen Press London

First published in Great Britain in 1994 by Andersen Press Ltd., 20 Vauxhall Bridge Road, London SW1V 2SA.
Published in Australia by Random House Australia Pty., 20 Alfred Street, Milsons Point, Sydney, NSW 2061. All
rights reserved. Colour separated in Switzerland by Photolitho AG, Offsetreproduktionen, Gossau, Zürich. Printed
and bound in Italy by Grafiche AZ, Verona.

10 9 8 7 6 5 4 3 2 1

British Library Cataloguing in Publication Data available.

ISBN 0 86264 484 4

This book has been printed on acid-free paper

"Grumpy? What's a Teddy Bear?"

I looked down. It was my granddaughter, Grace, and by her side crouched her little sister, Rebecca Scarlett, hardly off her knees, but sucking the hem of Grace's nose-high party dress.

"You mean you don't know what a Teddy Bear is?"

"No, I never saw a Teddy Bear and neither did Rebecca Scarlett, did you Rebecca Scarlett?"

Rebecca Scarlett looked up at her big sister and continued to suck the hem of her dress.

"Leave it to me," I said. "I'll go and find mine," and right away I climbed the stairs and rummaged through our large wardrobe where I keep all my bits and pieces and thingummyjigs which I am certain I will need again one day.

"That's strange," I thought, "I was certain Teddy would be right here with all my other precious bits and pieces. Teddy! Where are you?"

But there was no sign of Teddy anywhere. I looked and looked and made more and more mess. I even climbed inside the wardrobe just in case Teddy was hiding in a dark corner.

"We often used to play Hide-and-Seek together," I muttered from inside the wardrobe, "but it was a silly game really because I always knew where Teddy was hiding since I had put him there in the first place. Then whenever I went off to hide, Teddy could never come and look for me because he couldn't walk. He just used to sit there and wait to be hugged."

"How very puzzling," I groaned. Grace and Rebecca Scarlett were watching me expectantly as though at any moment I would produce Teddy magically from one of the funny hats or dented musical instruments lying strewn across the floor.

"I wonder if he is hiding in the attic where Teddy and I used to think a giant lived because it was so high up we couldn't reach it ourselves. I'll go and look," I said.

In a jiffy I was up the ladder and stumbling around a tangle of very old dusty rubbish that hadn't seen the light of day for a hundred years. But there was no sign of Teddy, or the giant for that matter, although I did come across his old brass dinner plate off which he used to eat very naughty children.

Grace and Rebecca Scarlett stood
at the bottom of the ladder looking
up through the dark hole in the
ceiling where their Grumpy had
disappeared.

"Perhaps Teddy has learned how to play real Hide-and-Seek at last," said Grace helpfully when I had got back down the ladder again.

"Perhaps," I said and went off to look down in the cellar where Teddy and I used to play Kidnapping and Hidden Treasure.

"I used to kidnap Teddy, tie his arms with a skipping rope, lock him in the cellar and demand a ransom," I explained. "My mum used to give me a biscuit and insist that I release Teddy at once, which I did so that Teddy and I could go and look for the Hidden Treasure. We never found any but I once found all my Christmas presents, which was the next best thing."

"Guess what," I said as I re-emerged from the cellar. "I haven't found Teddy, but I *have* found Teddy's left glass eye which I thought he had lost when we were playing pirates in an old washtub which my mum eventually filled with soil and put flowers in."

"Look, Grace," I said at last, "this is silly. Let's just go down to a toyshop and buy another Teddy."

Grace gave me a puzzled look and asked, "Why are they all called Teddy, Grumpy?"

"Well, er, because that's the name that Teddy Bears always have on the cardboard box they come in. Anyway, they always *look* like a Teddy so we call them Teddy. Let's go." So we did.

"A Teddy Bear?" said the shop assistant who
was busily trying out some of the new stock which
had just come in. "What's a Teddy Bear?"

"It's a golden brown fluffy sort of thing," I said, "and it looks just like a sad soul in a cardboard city."

"What's a cardboard city?" said the shop assistant.

"You're mad!" said the shop assistant. "Either you leave now or I'll call the manager!!"

"But I'm a customer," I said

"No you are not! You want something we do not stock, so you cannot be. Besides, everything in our shop is happy and colourful for happy and colourful children. We do not stock Teddy Bears with worn out sad faces who need to be loved, and we certainly do not stock Teddy Bears with worn out faces and only one eye in cheap and nasty cardboard boxes!"

"Well," I persisted, "do you stock Teddy Bears without cheap and nasty cardboard boxes, that come just as they are?"

"I'm going to call the manager," replied the shop assistant. And he did.

The manager appeared, and do you know what? He had a worn out face, looked awfully unloved and was exactly like my old Teddy Bear. And what's more, he had only one eye, so I bought him on the spot.

"Have you got a cardboard box?" I said.

"Hang on a minute," said the manager. "I'll get it and be with you in a tick." He started to rush off to the back of the shop, then stopped, turned and said, "Can I bring my friends? They really don't like it here either. Too much noise and not much fun. And don't worry. They'll be no trouble . . . and they've all got their own cardboard boxes too."

So they all came. Grace and Rebecca Scarlett had never been so happy . . . and neither had the Teddy Bears.